MYRO and the Railcar

Belongs to ....

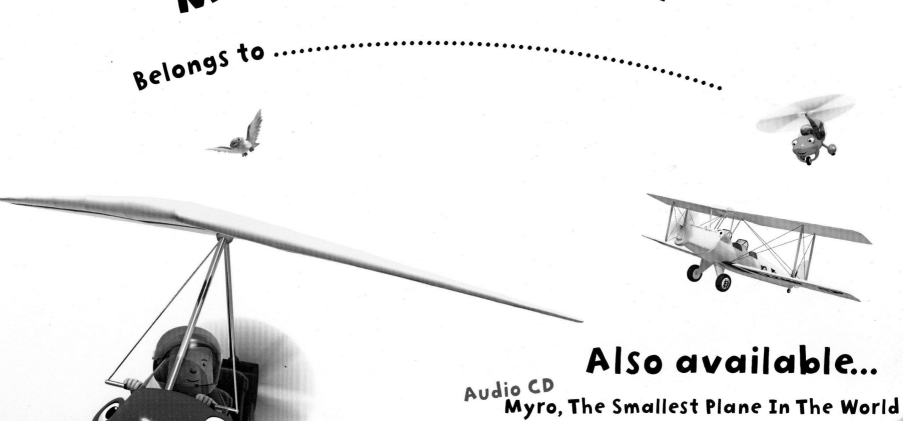

Also available...

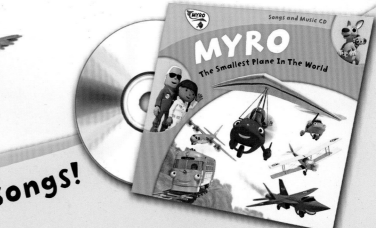

Myro and the Railcar
Book 4 from Series 1: Myro Goes to Australia

First published October 2010 by NickRose Ltd
www.nickrose.com
ISBN 978-1-907972-03-4

Myro's Team
Concept and Story: Nick Rose
Illustrations and Branding: Lucy Corrina Bourn
Designer: Sue Mason
Writer: Fiona Veitch Smith
Editor: Mary O'Riordan
Editorial Consultant: Samantha Mackintosh
Australian Consultant: Jane Massam
3D Consultancy: Jon Stuart and Sean Frisby
Project Management: Nick Rose
Continue the fun at www.myro.com

nr.
nickrose ltd

MYRO
and the
RAILCAR

Nick Rose

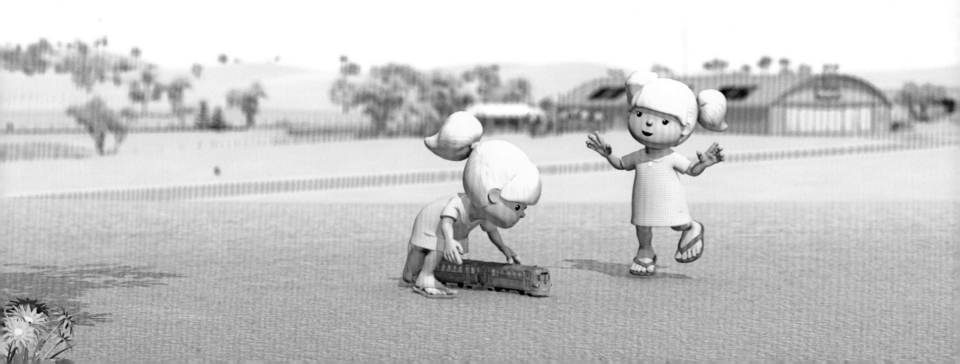

Myro the microlight is the smallest plane in the world!

He loves to fly in the
Australian Bush . . .

But his pilot was visiting Myro's home in the UK,
and so they hadn't been flying for weeks! Myro was getting grumpy.

"G'day, Myro," tooted Rayco, the very old and shiny diesel railcar that trundled past the flying club every day.
"How's my flying lawnmower today?"

"I'm **not** a lawnmower!"
Myro shouted back,
"I'm a super fast aeroplane!" and he
whirred his propeller in fury till the
dust flew up in a cloud around him.

Rayco also tooted at Tymo the Tiger Moth,
who had just been restored to his former glory.

"How ya goin', Tymo? Great to see you flying again!"

"Too right!" said the Tiger Moth.
"Us oldies can still do the job."

Myro was close to
moaning about
being grounded, when
Michael walked into the hangar.

"*Hooray!*" shouted Myro.
"You're back!" He raced over, shouting, "Let's go flying!"

Myro bounced from one wheel to the other,
desperate to get going.

"Calm down, Myro!" said the pilot.
"I've got a lot of things to do first."

Michael tramped off to the
clubhouse, while Myro looked on
crossly outside the hangar.

Tymo landed and taxied over to the little microlight.

"Why does Rayco make fun of me?" asked Myro.

"Aww, he's just pulling ya leg," said Tymo kindly.

"**Huh!** But he thinks he's **so** clever!" said
Myro moodily. "I'm much faster. I could beat him in
a race any day. He can only travel on rails, but I can fly anywhere!"

Tymo looked at his young friend sternly. "Rayco knows these mountains
much better than any of us," he warned.

But Myro had just had a naughty idea.

The next day Rayco trundled past and called, "How ya doin', little fella? Still not been flying? I hope you're not getting rusty!"

Myro was as mad as a maggot, so he decided to carry his idea out . . .

"Rayco's train driver said you were slower than an airship with a puncture," he fibbed to Michael.

"Ohhh, really?" Michael answered. "Well then, let's show him!" and he filled up Myro's fuel tank as fast as he could.

By the time Myro and his pilot were in the air, Rayco and his driver had had a long head start. But that didn't worry Myro. He knew he could catch up with the old railcar.

He zooommed through the air, following the railway line as it twisted and turned through the Blue Mountains.

Soon Myro spotted Rayco trundling up the middle zig-zag.

Myro dropped as low as he could and flew beside the railcar.

The passengers all rushed to the windows to wave at him.

The little microlight tipped his wing to the left, then to the right, and smiled back at them.

Rayco tooted loudly, but didn't seem pleased to see Myro.

Toot! Toot!

"Huh!" said Myro. "I'll show him how fast I can fly. He'll never call me a lawnmower again!"

And he zipped off at full throttle, leaving Rayco tooting frantically on his air horn . . .

Toot! Toot! Toot! Toot!

Myro was enjoying showing off.
He was hoping that everyone was looking at him.

Rayco carried on tooting louder,
and *louder*
and *louder.*

But Myro ignored him
and picked up more speed instead.

He followed the railway track round
a bend, past a station
and into a cutting.

But as he rushed between the
rock walls, he saw the railway ended
in front of him at the bottom of
a steep cliff face!

Disaster!

"HELP!" yelled Myro,
his engine spluttering in sudden fright.

Myro pushed his wing forward
and flew upwards so fast his engine
almost screamed off his airframe!

His wheels nearly touched
the cliff face as he climbed
higher and higher.

Myro was terrified he
wouldn't make it to the top . . .

Then suddenly – **whoooooosh!**

– the little microlight came up into open sky!

"Phewee!"

He'd missed the cliff by a wallaby's whisker,
and was trembling with fright.

Myro landed on the cliff top, gasping for air.

TOOT! TOOT!

Down below, Rayco was chugging
towards the top zig-zag,
still blowing his whistle . . .

Toot!
Toot!

. . . and Myro realised something.
"Rayco was trying to warn us," he murmured, feeling awful
about the way he'd behaved.
"We'd better get down there and say sorry," said Michael.
His voice was shaking as much as Myro's wing.

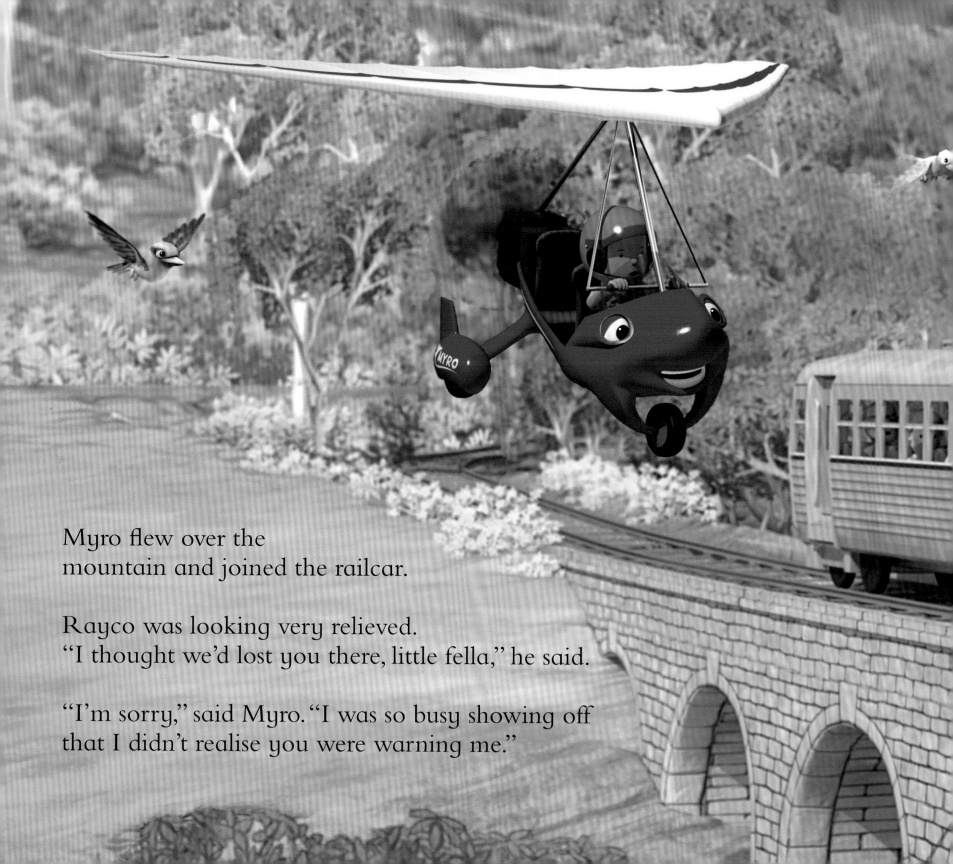

Myro flew over the
mountain and joined the railcar.

Rayco was looking very relieved.
"I thought we'd lost you there, little fella," he said.

"I'm sorry," said Myro. "I was so busy showing off
that I didn't realise you were warning me."

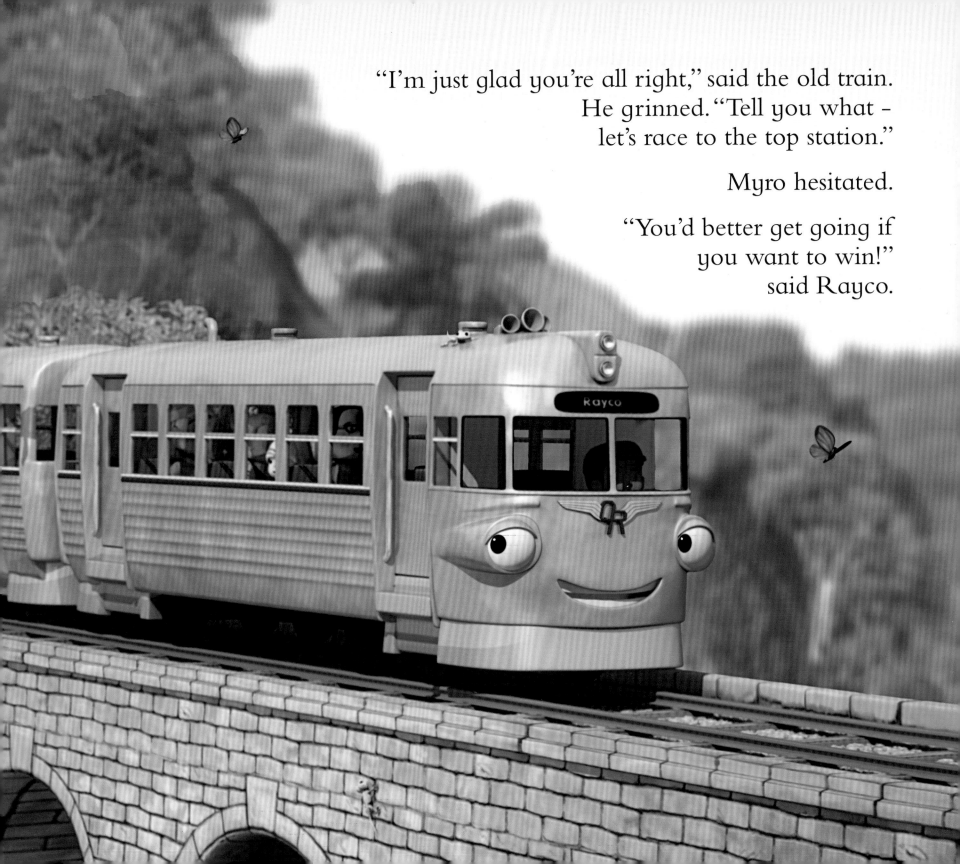

"I'm just glad you're all right," said the old train. He grinned. "Tell you what – let's race to the top station."

Myro hesitated.

"You'd better get going if you want to win!" said Rayco.

But funnily enough Myro didn't feel like racing. This time, he had a better idea.

"Can you tell me about the Blue Mountains?" said Myro.
"Tymo says you know this place better than anyone."

So the old railcar and the young microlight went home together –
chatting about everything from bandicoot bottoms and possum poo,
to weirdy wallaroos and crazy kangaroos . . .

. . . and lawnmowers were never mentioned again!

Signalman's Phonetic Alphabet

A	Alpha	**N**	November
B	Bravo	**O**	Oscar
C	Charlie	**P**	Papa
D	Delta	**Q**	Quebec
E	Echo	**R**	Romeo
F	Foxtrot	**S**	Sierra
G	Golf	**T**	Tango
H	Hotel	**U**	Uniform
I	India	**V**	Victor
J	Juliet	**W**	Whisky
K	Kilo	**X**	X-ray
L	Lima	**Y**	Yankee
M	Mike	**Z**	Zulu